SECRETS OF A SUGAR BABY 2

SUGAR BABY SECRETS BOOK 2

MIA BLACK

CHAPTER 1

Jae

The steam rose into the air as he fondled me in the shower. He slid his hands down to my backside as the water splashed off our skin. I giggled when his lips brushed against my neck. "Blake, you are so bad, but honestly, I love that though. I absolutely love it."

I looked through the foggy glass at the things in the bathroom. The marble countertops sat on top of the black tiles. The vanity bulbs around the mirror had to be for his wife. Blake was fine as hell, but I knew that he wasn't particular about the details of his appearance. I glanced towards the door and that was when I saw a foggy figure standing near the door. I squinted my eyes in that direction. "Um, Blake? I think there is somebody standing at the door."

"Huh?" he removed his lips off my neck and looked at the figure near the door. Moments later, he pulled the shower door open and rushed outside.

I saw her clearly. She stood with her arms folded over her chest and her head tilted to the left as if she was trying to get a better view of what was going on. Her long, blonde hair had been pulled into a ponytail. Her designer jeans hugged her hips and her form fitting top did little to conceal her bust. She turned around and left the bathroom as Blake trailed behind her as he tried to keep his footing on the black tile.

I sucked my teeth and turned off the shower head, then exited and wrapped a towel around my body. I couldn't even be mad about the situation because I knew he was married. I knew what I was getting into from the jump, but I just hadn't seen her until now. To me, she didn't exist until today. I wiped the glass clear from the fog and glanced at myself in the mirror. I should be the one living in this mansion with him. She didn't deserve him or his wealth and, if she did, he wouldn't have been messing around with me.

Outside, I could hear the chatter of an argument brewing. As soon as I opened the bathroom door, the voices became louder. I exhaled, then walked to the master bedroom to grab my clothes. It was time for me to go. I didn't want any issues with her while I was here and I figured that now was the best time for me to leave.

I slid into my pants one leg at a time, then hopped around so that I could pull them above my waist. As soon as I snapped the buckle, I heard a door slam closed. Seconds later, I heard him speak to me as I pulled my shirt down over my chest. "Where are you going?"

I wrinkled my eyebrows together. "Are you serious? You really want to ask me that right now when your wife is outside? For all I know, she could be going out to the car to get a pistol and then come back in here and shoot us both."

He scoffed at the idea. "Her? Yeah right. She is not going to do anything like that. That woman has never held a pistol in her life. She is not that type of person."

He stepped closer to me. "You never know what people are capable of when they are upset. People have been killed in moments of passion. I don't want to put myself in that position. Besides, you shouldn't want me here anyway. You should probably be trying to fix things with her before she comes back in here."

He wrapped his arms around me and then walked me to the window. He pulled back the curtain and pointed outside. She had just backed her BMW down the driveway and burned rubber from in front of the house. "See? What did I tell you? She is upset, but she will get over it. She knows what the deal is here."

I faced him, still in his arms. "The deal? What is the deal? How about you fill me in on that."

He kissed me on the lips, but I turned away before his tongue could slide inside of my mouth. He smiled. "Alright. Jae, we have an open marriage. I smash who I want, when I want, and she does the same. Sometimes, we do it together. I mean, that is rare because she is hardly in the mood for it, but it has happened more than a handful of times over the years we have been married."

Something didn't seem right about that. I didn't think that they would argue if this open marriage thing was agreed upon by the both of them. But, I guess they could've had details to it or a line that he crossed with having me here when she was in town. I didn't know, but it just didn't seem as simple as he claimed it to be.

"Come on, don't leave, baby. Stay here. I'll have my chef whip us up a nice breakfast and we can finish out our morning together. What do you think?"

"I don't know. What if your wife comes back while we are eating? Then what?"

He laughed. "Trust me, she won't be back today. I made sure of it." He left my side, the walked over to grab some jogging pants to cover his lower half. His valor housecoat draped off his naked body and, even though I wanted to leave, I couldn't. His streaky blue eyes made it hard for me to turn away from him. After he finished getting dressed, he extended his hand towards me. A gold necklace danced around his deck as he waited patiently for me to connect with him.

Finally, I rolled my eyes and walked by him. "I am not holding your hand though."

He slapped me on my behind as I walked past. "Oh, you're feisty now, huh? You know how I like that kind of stuff."

I smiled as I walked ahead of him and down the winding stairs, then into his spacious kitchen. A chef stood at the stove, scrambling eggs in a skillet as if nothing had happened between Blake and his wife. He smiled at me just as Blake entered the room behind me. "Alonzo, the usual, please?"

"Right away, sir. Should I make double for your guest?"

"Yes, please. Make one extra of everything."

Blake pulled my chair out for me at the large, circular dining room table. He sat down right beside me and put his hand on top of my thigh. "I can't believe you were going to leave. Alonzo makes the best breakfast on this side of the moon. You have to try it."

"Yeah, I am. But, I'm not going to stay here long. That whole situation with your wife rubbed me the wrong way."

I didn't want to admit my jealousy. I had to play it off like it was something other than that. He told me upfront what it was with me, but to me, things had started taking a turn. Blake was everything a woman would want. Fine as hell, wealthy and with a dope sex game. I couldn't ask for much more and I'm not sure if any other woman could, either. If I had to guess, he was probably the one who tabled the idea of an open marriage and she had to go along with it. Either that, or risk losing him to a woman who wouldn't put up a fight about it. That would be like throwing away a winning lottery ticket. No woman was that stupid, but in the back of my mind, I hoped she was.

The chef finished our breakfast. Bacon, egg and cheese omelets with salmon croquettes, buttered toast and jelly on the side. I had to admit that if it tasted as good as it smelled, it just might be the best breakfast I'd ever had. I sliced into the omelet and cheese oozed out of the opening. Blake smiled as he looked on. "What did I tell you? He knows what he is doing. He is worth that $600 an hour price tag. I'd pay that two times over."

We ate our meal and the whole time, I felt like his wife would barge back in with a pistol, ready to blow our heads off. But, as time went by, she never showed up. There was no sign of her. After I finished, I looked at Blake. He had already completed his meal by the time our eyes locked with each other. "I think I am going to head home now."

"So soon? Really? I figured we would spend a little more time together."

"I just don't want to be here when she shows up again. I don't like competition."

"Competition? No, she knows her role. Trust me, the last thing you have to worry about is her coming back in here to start some mess. The most you will see out of her is what you saw earlier. Just a grown woman throwing a hissy fit. That's it."

"What was it about?"

He sighed. "Nothing. It was nothing. She just has some other things going on right now, that's all."

I didn't believe him for a second. I stood up and thanked the chef for the meal, then Blake walked me to the door. The sunlight beamed down on us as we stood outside his front door. "So," he said, smiling, "when am I going to see you again?"

"I don't know. You have my number and you know where I am at. Whenever you want to see me, you will make it happen."

"Yeah. You know I will, baby. I hate you have to leave, but I get it. Until next time?"

He kissed me on the lips and with that, I left his home and headed back to my side of town. I hated leaving his mansion just to go back down to the gutter where I was from. I think that was why I wanted to stay with him. I knew what he could offer me, and I wasn't sure if I would be able to find that with anyone else.

As soon as I got home, I shook my head. My aunt was sitting on the couch in the living room as I slammed the door closed behind me. "What are you doing here? You need to get up and get out. I don't have time for your mess anymore."

"Wait, Jae. Just hold on a minute, alright?"

"Hold on for what? I don't need to hold on to anything, you just need to get up and get out of my house. I told you to be gone by the time I came back."

She scooted to the edge of the couch. "Please, Jae. I left. I really did, but I had to come back. My boyfriend Melvin. He beat me up and raped me on top of that. I had to leave. I had to get away from him because he was liable to kill me, Jae. Please. I don't have anywhere else to go."

Her lip was puffy, and her eye had been blackened. I knew there was a chance she could've gotten beat up by Melvin, but there was also a chance that she got into a fight over some drugs in the street again. It wouldn't have been the first time something like that happened. I hated taking her in because it was just a matter of time before she started stealing my things and selling them on the street just to get her next high.

"Listen, Angie, I am only going to tell you this once. If you stay here, I swear to God, the moment I find any of my things missing, or that you are here getting high in my home? You are out and I don't care if you can't find a pot to piss in or a pillow to sleep on. You are gone."

"Thank you, Jae. Thank you so much and I promise you that I won't cause you any trouble. That is my word."

I sucked my teeth, then walked by her and into my room. She had said the same thing to me many times before just to pull the rug out from under my feet. I wasn't going to allow it to happen again.

CHAPTER 2

Blake

I paced back and forth in the front room, trying to figure out how my wife came home to find me and Jae in the shower. I made plans for her to be out of town, but for some reason, she hadn't gone. That led to her catching me in the middle of everything with Jae. I wasn't worried about losing her, though, because this wasn't the first time she had caught me.

I had been cheating on her since the day the agency sent her over to me. She got mad the first few times, but after that, she seemed to take it all in stride. The only reason I rushed out of the bathroom after her was because I didn't want her to say anything to Jae that would tip her off to my cheating. As long as she believed that I was in an open marriage, I had nothing to worry about. I just hoped that she stuck with the thought and I had to make sure she understood that an open marriage is exactly what it was.

If I could be honest with myself, I would prefer a woman with a backbone. Someone who would get mad and perhaps throw things when they caught me in the act. Maybe that would go further to change my behavior, but it seemed like the women put up with my cheating just because I had bank. It is the same thing with the pro athletes that cheat on their wives. They hardly ever get divorced because that much is expected to happen. The men cheat and, since we are wealthy, they chose to put up with it. The prenuptial agreement helps, too. I made sure to have that drawn up just like I did in my previous marriage so, just in case we did decide to split, they couldn't take half of shit from me. This was my fortune that I built with my own hands and I'll be damned if a woman came in and took it out of my grasp. That would never happen.

Almost thirty minutes went by before Carissa came back home. She closed the front room door as I looked at her. She didn't say a word to me. She tossed the keys on the table, then her footsteps echoed as she walked down the hallway towards the stairs. I admired her from behind and soon after that, I followed her up and to our room.

"Is she gone?" she asked as she untied her hair.

"Yeah. She left a while ago. But, what are you doing here? You were supposed to be out of town."

"Oh, that is how you planned it, huh?" She placed her hair tie on the dresser. "Well, isn't that grand? You made sure I would be out of town so you could do what you please. It was a good idea, however, I didn't feel like going anymore, so I decided to come home—just to find my husband in the shower with some ghetto whore."

"Come on now, Carissa, don't act like this is something new, and there is no need for name calling."

She spun towards me. "Oh, so you don't like when I call her names, huh? Well, I don't care what you don't like. I call a spade a spade and, from the looks of her, she is nothing more than a little hood rat skank hoe."

She was trying to trigger me and I knew it. I laughed at her attempt. She wasn't one to curse much and when she did, she sounded awkward. The words never left her lips the way they were supposed to. For the most part, she seemed like she was ok with the way I had been treating her. That, in itself, was a turnoff to me.

"Look, I know you feel a way about what I am doing, but it is what it is. Don't get me wrong, I appreciate you and everything you do for me, but what you are to me is simple. You are here for appearance. You are the woman I call when I need to go out to an engagement and impress a certain caliber of people. Your beauty. The way you carry yourself. You are the type of woman I want people to see on my arm. However, that is all you are here for. These other women? I want them for other things. They satisfy my lust in ways that you are not designed to. They are here for fun, you are here for business. That is the difference."

She stood in front of the mirror quietly as if she was still digesting everything I said. She needed to know the truth. This marriage was not the typical one. I sat down on the bed and waited for her to respond, but instead, she continued untying her hair just to tie it back into a bun. I watched her walk past me and into the walk-in closet where she grabbed a bag and began placing things inside of it.

I exhaled. "So, where are you going now?"

"I am going to the condo. I need to have some time to myself right now, so, that is where I will be if you need to contact me. But," she continued placing things into her bag, "can you answer one question for me?"

"Yes."

"Do you love her?"

"Who? Jae? Hell no I don't love that girl. Like I told you before, she is just here for lust. To fulfill desires that you aren't able to. That is all this is about."

I was lying through my teeth, but she would never know the truth. The fact is, I didn't love her, but I liked Jae a lot more than any other woman at any point in my life. She was everything to me, but, I just couldn't see myself settling down with someone like her. Her attitude. Besides that, she was far too young for me. She was built for me to have fun with and nothing more. At least, that was what I tried to convince myself.

She lingered as she looked into my eyes and finally, she responded. "Alright. If you say so, then I have no choice but to believe you. But, you said her name was Jae, right?"

"Yes."

"Hmm." She looked away from me for a moment, then

nodded her head. "Alright. That is all I needed to know. I am headed to the condo should you need me."

"Ok."

I reclined in the bed as she carried her bags out of the room. I couldn't care less that she was leaving and, if it was up to me, she would've been gone a long time ago. I grabbed my phone and scrolled through the pictures that Jae had sent me. Half-naked pictures that would hold me over until the next time we would meet again. She was built exactly the way I liked them. Thick below the waist and not much up top. I was always told that anything more than a mouthful was just a waste.

I sent her a text message, then got up to get into the shower. I hated that she had to leave so soon, and I knew I had to make it up to her. After I got out the shower, she had already sent a response. "Hey. I am just sitting here in my bed. What's up?"

I snapped a picture of myself as I stood in front of the mirror in my bedroom. I stood at an angle that complimented the muscles in my chest and the sculped abs in my mid-section. I pressed send on the picture, then followed it up with a text. "I just wanted to apologize for ending our morning session earlier than we wanted to. I really wish that you had stayed a little longer."

"Damn. Yeah, I will be saving this picture for good. But, I just didn't want to be there. I guess the mood was kind of thrown off whenever your um—your wife showed up. So, I just needed some time to myself. Besides, isn't she there? You may need to give your attention to her now."

I shook my head, laughing at her response. If she didn't have a salty ass comment to say, I think I wouldn't have believed it was her. "That woman is just here for show. Nothing more, nothing less."

"Ok. Well, I know one way you can make this better. I need a new purse, anyway."

"Lol—alright. Say no more."

I laid on the bed and then signed into my bank account online so I could transfer money into her checking. It was just another way that I apologized for whatever I did to her. It was easy, but it was worth it, especially if she was still going to put up with me after it was all said and done. A small price to pay for her loyalty.

CHAPTER 3

Jae

It was the fifth time he tried to get me to come back over since the day I left his house after breakfast. I didn't want anything to do with him right now. I was still bothered by the fact that his wife popped up on us. He had been sending $5,000 transfers to my bank account for the past four days to try to lure me over to his place. I took the money, happily, but I still didn't plan on going anywhere near him. Annoyed, I answered the phone.

"Hello?"

"Jae, what's up, baby? Why have you been so distant over the past few days?"

I exhaled and sat against my headboard. "I'm just tired. I've been on my period and when that starts, I just don't feel doing anything."

"Oh—you're on your period?"

I was lying, but that was the only way to get him off my back. I knew all he wanted to do was have sex and I just wasn't in the mood to do anything like that with him right now. "Yeah. It just started a couple of days ago."

"Oh, I see. Well, alright then. I guess I'll let you deal with that, but honestly, I still want to see you. It doesn't always have to be about sex between us. I know it is good, but to be honest, I love your company. The way you make me feel, you know? These types of feelings don't come around often."

"I understand. But, I'm not up to it right now. I will give you a call or text you when I am ready to get out again."

"Ok."

I knew he was dejected, but I didn't care. I had to figure out how to clear my mind and as soon as we hung up the phone, I got into the shower so I could get dressed and go out on a shopping spree to spend some of the money that he had been sending me for the past few days. After I got out of the shower, I called Shayla to see what she was doing. I figured it would be a good time to spend with my girl so she could help me get my mind off some things.

"Hey, Shayla. You busy?"

"Nah, boo, I'm free. What's up?"

"I just need to get out for a minute. I need somebody to talk to so I was hoping you could meet up with me somewhere."

"Yeah. I'm already out shopping right now. You want to meet me up here at the mall, or did you have somewhere else in mind?"

"Nah, I can meet you up there. Give me like thirty minutes."

"Take your time. I'll be here for a minute."

I hung up the phone and got dressed so I could meet her up there. I don't know why this was bugging me so much, but I hated feeling like the side chick. I already knew what the deal was when I first met Blake, but for some reason, it was like seeing his wife had changed things for me. I needed to talk with someone to get through this.

"Damn, baby. Let me holla at you for a minute. Shit, you fine as hell!"

I ignored men's cat calls as I walked to the front door of the mall. The revolving door spun around as soon as I stepped inside. People walked around the mall with bags in their hands, smiling as they enjoyed spending their money on the things their hearts desired. I headed up the steps. I didn't even need to call Shayla. I knew she would be in the Gucci store. She lived there.

As soon as I stepped into the store, I saw her at the purse rack, scanning through the totes one by one. "Ok," she said to the store clerk, "I want this one. Can you unchain it or do whatever the hell you gotta do to take it off the rack? Thank you."

The clerk stuck his key in the lock and popped it open. I waited until she spun around to see me standing in the entrance. "Oh, heeeey, boo! You just knew I was up in here givin' Gucci all my lil' coins, huh?"

"Yeah. You are the only person I know that still shops here religiously."

"Yeah, I ain't about trends and you know that. Once I find something I like, I stick with it until I find something better. Better has not showed up at my doorstep yet though."

She got me to crack a smile for the first time in a few days. My aunt had been bugging me ever since she showed up. I couldn't take my mind off the thought that she was stealing things out of my place in the middle of the night. I was afraid that I would wake up to half of my things gone. I brought every piece of electronics and every other valuable thing in the room with me and locked my bedroom door at night. I couldn't chance anything like that happening.

I waited patiently for Shayla to check out of the line and after she got her purse, we walked out of the store. She had on stilettos and a black maxi dress. It didn't matter what time of day it was, or where we were at, she always made sure that she was dressed to perfection. I knew she just did it for attention, but that didn't matter to me.

We walked through the mall as men's eyes glued to us on the way past. Shayla carried on as if it was normal for her. We made it to the food court and sat down at one of the tables in the middle of the room. She pulled her phone out of her purse. Her lips were coated with a light layer of gloss and her breasts were pushed together in the middle of her chest.

"I swear Anthony is doin' everything he can so slide between these legs. Nigga got me fucked up though, that's what I know. He ain't touchin' this cooter. Not at all." She put the phone down, smiling, as she looked at me. "But, later for that nigga. What's up with you, boo? Why did you need an emergency meeting with me? Something goin' on?"

"Yeah." I exhaled and thought about Blake. I didn't know why it was weighing on my so hard, but I couldn't get the thought out of my mind. I didn't want his wife in the picture at all. I told her what happened a few days ago. How she caught us in the shower and didn't hardly make a scene after that. "He said he is in an open marriage."

"Open marriage? Like, he can fuck whoever he wants? And she can, too?"

"Yeah, that's what I took it as. But, I don't know. She didn't snap or anything, but, the way he ran out of the bathroom after her made me think it was something else. Like, if they have an open marriage, why would he have to run out after her? And I heard them arguing while I was getting dressed. None of it makes sense to me."

"Damn. Open marriage, huh? Shit, if I ever do decide to settle down, I might have to look into that option. That is the best of both fuckin' worlds. Literally. Got the main nigga right at the crib and whenever I see somethin' else I wanna smash, then I am free to do it. Shit. That sounds like a plan to me."

I tilted my head to the side. "Shayla? Can we remain focused here? Please?"

"Yeah, yeah, my bad. Ok, so, she walked in on yall when yall were in the shower. Then she got mad and walked out and that's it?"

"Yeah."

"Well, you know what I think about that. Shit, I don't give a damn about no other hoes, you know what I'm sayin'? How much is he cashin' you out with?"

"He has given me almost 10 racks in the last few days."

"Damn. Shit, with that much money, I don't care what he told me. He could be married in ten different stated with ten different women. As long as he is givin' me that bread, that is all that matters and that is all that matters to you. Just meet yo' obligations with him. Fuck him, suck him and keep it movin'. This shit you are talkin' about right now means nothing. It shouldn't mean anything, anyway. You know what it sound like though? It sounds like you startin' to catch feeling for him."

"What? Nah. I ain't catchin' feelings for him."

"You gotta be. That's the only other reason why you would say anything about him having another chick around."

"Nah, it ain't that. I mean, I knew he was married off top. It's just—"

"Just what, Jae? Just that you startin' to like this dude, right? You startin' to let yo' heart get involved in a business affair? Shit, please don't tell me that is what you are doing. Please don't tell me that shit."

"Nah, it ain't it. I'm tellin' you it ain't that. I just felt weird when the bitch saw me in the shower with her man. That's all it is. I'm serious."

She pushed her mouth to the side. I knew she didn't believe me because shit, I didn't believe myself. I was starting to get too attached to Blake and I knew it. Maybe taking some time away from him would be a good thing. I hadn't seen him in a few days and for right now, at least, I thought it was best if I kept it that way.

After we finished lunch, there was still something missing in me and I couldn't explain it. I decided that I would go and visit Darryl. It had been a while since I seen him last. He had gone off to college to play basketball and I'd always thought of him like a brother. That had been our relationship in the past. It seemed like he turned into something more than that though. More like a best friend. Somebody that I could talk to about anything. He didn't know what I was involved in back at home and I wanted to keep it that way. I couldn't have him looking at me any different. I booked a flight to visit him the next day. I wanted to surprise him on campus.

When I got there, I could feel the young energy. Students walking around campus with bookbags, grouped together in small huddles. A group of girls stood off to the side wearing pink and green clothing. Pretty girls. They had to be a part of a sorority. Across from them beneath a few trees in the grass, another group of girls wearing all red with triangles on their clothing. *Deltas*.

I thought about which sorority I would have joined if I went this path in life. There was no telling, though. I was far too gone to even think about something like that. I walked down the pathway, breezing past men as they twirled red and white canes around in their hands and just beyond them, big, black sexy ass men with gold boots looked as if they were unchained dogs, ready to attack at any given moment.

A few of them barked at me as I walked by, smiling, until I made it to Darryl's dorm. I remembered his room number from our conversations we had when the year started. He had always tried to get me to come and visit him, but I was too busy to break away and see what he wanted to show me. Now, I had time and I needed to get away, so this was the perfect opportunity for me.

I found his number and knocked on the door. All I had with me was a duffle bag with enough things to last me for another day. I didn't plan on staying long. Just enough to show my face and try to let go of the cloudiness that was in my mind. The door pulled open. Darryl smiled ear-to-ear when he saw me standing in front of him.

"Damn! Jae? Is that really you!? Shit! Is this real?"

I smiled. "Yes, nigga, this is real." I stepped in for a hug and he embraced me tight like he had been waiting for this moment for a long time.

"Damn. I swear I never would've guessed that it would be you knocking on this door and shit. Damn." We released each other. "Well, shit, come in. I was about to go get something to eat, but I can wait for a little bit. When did you get here?"

I stepped inside and he took the duffle bag off my shoulder and tossed it to the side near the couch. "I just got here like thirty minutes ago. My plane landed and I caught an Uber to get here."

"No shit? Damn. I mean, it is good to see you." We sat down on the couch and he examined me as if he knew something was up. I could feel it between us. Something was different and I think we both knew it. "So, I see you are still fine as shit. What brings you out here?"

"I just came to visit you. I know you are surprised that I remembered your dorm room and the number."

"Hell yeah I am. I am surprised that you are here altogether. I mean, when I hit you up earlier about it, I never thought that you would show up. You kept sayin' how busy you were, so I just left it alone."

"Yeah, I am still busy with work and stuff like that, but, I found a little time to get away. So, I just decided to drop in on you and see how you were doing. How the basketball shit is going for you, you know?"

"I feel you. Well, yeah, I'm glad to see you, for real." The smile never left his lips. "But yo', come on. You can come with me to get something to eat and I can show you around and shit. Show you where I practice and everything. Introduce you to some of the homies."

"Yeah. Yeah, I'd like that." We exchanged smiles with each other for a few moments before we both stood to our feet. He grabbed a black and gold jacket and tossed it on. "You pledged?"

"Yeah. Alpha Phi Alpha. I didn't plan on it, but when I got out here, I saw that I was cool with a lot of the niggas that were in that frat, so I did some research on it and found it that it was for me. So, I jumped right in."

"I see. That black and gold looks good on you though."

"I appreciate it."

He closed the door behind us and with that, we made our way down the hall and back onto the campus. People called out to him as we walked the pathway. He nodded his head while I walked inches away from him. He shook hands with some and dapped others. "Damn, I see you are just Mr. Popularity around here."

"Nah, it's just the basketball shit. Most of the athletes get love like that, especially if you are halfway decent. I mean, I am here on scholarship, so, they already expect a lot of me. I am just fortunate enough to live up to expectations so far. Hold on, these are the fellas right here. I want you to meet them."

He walked me over to a group of men who all dawned a similar version of the jacket he had on. "Peace, fam," one of them said as they shook his hand with his eyes on me. "And who is this beautiful queen you have with you?"

"Yo', this is the one I been tellin' yall about. Jae."

His eyebrows lifted to the middle of his forehead as he smiled at me. "Oh, so this is Jae, huh? Damn. It feels like I already know you the way this nigga talks about you. Every other word, it's 'Jae this and Jae that.' I mean, he says that yall are like brother and sister, buuuut I don't know. That shit is kinda suspect because as much as I love my sister, I don't talk about her half as much as he talks about you."

His friends laughed with each other and shook hands in agreement with what was just said. Darryl looked at me and shook his head with a smirk clinging to the corner of his mouth. "Nah, it ain't like that. I don't talk about you on that level. You are a good friend and I just wanted MY BOYS," he said, looking at them, "to know about you. That's all."

"Well, Ms. Jae, even though I feel like I already know

you, it is a pleasure to finally put a face with the name." He looked at Darryl, "what yall about to get into?"

"Just bout to take her to the center to get somethin' to eat and then show her where we hoop at and shit."

"Awww, a little campus date," he said as his frat brother laughed behind him."

"Ha ha, niggas, real funny. See what I get for introducing my brothers to my best friend?"

"Best friend? Oh, shit, yo' best friend? She yo' best friend now? What happened to sister?" Darryl paused. "Oh, I know why you switched it. Because it is mad freaky if you end up doin' yo' thang with her when you claim her as yo' sister, but if you call her yo' best friend, then that shit is wide open now. Yeah, I feel you, my nigga! I feel you!"

They laughed and shook hands with each other. Darryl looked at me, smiling. "You ready?"

I nodded my head, then spoke to them. "It was a pleasure meeting yall."

"You too, queen."

We walked away from the group of men. "Sorry about

that," Darryl said, "they can be some clowns sometimes."

"Nah, it's cool. I ain't trippin' off that. But, I am a little surprised that you talked about me that much. I wasn't expecting to hear that."

"Yeah," he said as he looked straight ahead. It seemed as if he was too shy to tell me what he wanted to say while looking my way. "You are special to me. We have known each other for a while, and you have always been close to me heart. Always."

"Really? Damn. Honestly, I can say the same thing about you. Why else would I catch a plane and come out here to see you on the spur of the moment?"

"Maybe you killed somebody, and you are trying to hide out somewhere for a few days."

I laughed as he opened the center door for me. "Shit, if I did that, this would be the last place I would go. I'm pretty sure I would've been on the first thing smokin' out of the US."

"Oh, so you got a plan, huh?"

"I always have a plan."

I winked at him, then we went inside the center and got

something to eat. As we enjoyed our meal, I couldn't help the feelings that start bubbling in my heart for him. I always knew I cared about Darryl, but right now, things were different. We were older and a lot more mature than we were during the days we knew each other growing up. His beard stretched a couple inches off the sides of his face. The hair wasn't curly. It was straight and fine. The evidence that he had a little bit of Puerto Rican blood in him. His deep, wavy hair was another thing, but the way his eyes slanted, and his eyebrows thickened above his eyes. Physically, he was everything for me. Everything that I could see myself with later down the line.

"You barely touched your burger. Were you hungry?"

"Nah, not really. I mean, I had a bite to eat on the plane ride, so I guess I am still full from that."

"Ok. Well, shit, I ain't gon' make you eat nothin'. It ain't like we at yo' mom's house when we were little. You remember she used to make us sit there until we ate everything off our plates."

"Hell yeah—and you would try to spread all your food around to make it look like you ate yo' shit, but then she would come to you and push it all back together."

"Niggas had HELLA food left on the plate!"

We laughed together. It had been a while since I was able to let myself go and enjoy the moment. Back home, it was always work, hustle, fuck, cash out and keep it movin'. Talking to Darryl slowed things down for me. Made me appreciate the small things in life and enjoy the moments as they came. I wished that I could take this frame of mind back to D.C. with me, but I knew that wouldn't be the case.

We got up from the table and then he showed me around his campus. The basketball court where he played and practiced, the hallway where all the former standout players had their jersey's retired. The whole time he talked to me, I undressed him with my eyes. I slowly took his shirt off and then removed his pants from his 6'5" frame. His muscles bulged on his chest. I wanted him. I wanted him now more than ever.

After we finished, we went back to his dorm room. "Well, shit, it is only one tiny ass bed here, so, if you don't want to be squeezed up with me on that twin, then you can take the bed and I can take the couch. It's all good."

"Boy, why are you actin' like that? Like we ain't slept in

the same type of twin bed together when we were little. You better stop treatin' me like a stranger before I snap."

He laughed. "Shit, my bad. I didn't know if you had a man back at the crib or not, you feel me? I just wanted to be respectful."

I thought about the men that I had been messing around with in D.C., primarily Blake. We weren't in a relationship, but he was the closest thing I had to one and that wasn't saying much at all. "Nah, I am single, so you don't have anything to worry about."

"Cool. Well, shit, I'm about to hop in the shower. You can relax. The remote is right there. Make yourself at home."

"Ok."

I watched him walk into the bathroom and close the door behind him. I grabbed my bag and went into his room to put on my bed clothes: some boy shorts and a loose-fitting wife-beater. The kind that my titties would end up slipping out of by the end of the night. Ten minutes went by before he got out of the shower and saw me beneath the covers in his bed. "You must be tired."

"You had me walking around the campus all evening. It is almost 10 pm and I am getting sleepy."

"Well, I ain't gon' stop you from fallin' asleep. And shit, if you're in the bed, then so am I." He climbed into the bed next to me. I could tell he was a little nervous about where he could put his hands, so I grabbed one of them and placed it firmly over my breast. He scooted his body closer to me as I arched my backside into him. "Oh, ok. We can do it like this, too."

I held his hand over my breast and stroked the back of his hand. "Do you miss what we used to have? The friendship?"

"Yeah. Yeah, I miss that shit. You can tell by the way I talk about you out here. I know my brothers were just trying to get the jokes off, but I really do miss you. I talk about you probably way more than I should. Like, stalkerish, I guess."

"Nah, it's cool. It ain't really stalkerish, either. I think about you, too, I just can't talk about you as freely as you can talk about me. I mean, not like that—I just," I realized I had probably told him too much. I left doors open for him to ask questions that I probably wasn't ready to answer. "I just miss you and I'll leave it at that."

"Yeah. I miss you too."

He held me closer. I could feel his heart beat into my back. I moved his hand to my lips and kissed the back of it slowly. Then again. Then one more time. I felt his dick poke me in my ass. I closed my eyes. I knew it was about to happen and I would've been lying if I said I didn't want it to. I turned to face him and put my hand on his chest, then moved my lips towards his. We connected in a sea of passion. His hand slid down to my backside and grabbed a handful of my cheeks.

"Do what you want to me," I whispered to him in a small space between our lips.

I reached my hand down and felt it, moaning at the thought of all of that going inside of me. My panties were drenched by the time he pulled my pants over my hips. He slid his tongue on my inner thigh, licking until he reached my pussy. I put my hand on the top of his head as he used his hands to spread my legs further. My breathing increased as soon as his tongue stroked my clit. I clenched the couch cushion in my fists as he flicked his tongue back and forth like a snake, sending waves of ecstasy through my body. I panted, trying to catch my breath, but feeling as though I forgot how to breathe.

His muscles flexed as he held my legs in place. I moaned in a falsetto once his tongue hit my stiff clitoris and sent a wall of water rushing from inside me like the levies had just been broken. "Right there, right there. Yes, yeeesss!"

He swirled his tongue, folding it over and making it turn flips inside of my pussy. I pounded the mattress. "Ooh, yes, baby, just like that. Just like that." He looked up at me, smiling, then dove back in for another round. I damn near blacked out from pleasure before he stopped and climbed on top of me.

I heard papers rustle below me as my eyes were closed. Suddenly, he stood up and moments later, I felt a long, stiff dick sliding into me. My mouth opened, wanting to scream out in ecstasy, but not able to find the words to release. He drove his penis inside of me as he pushed my legs back of my head. I hadn't been stretched out like this in a long time. My titties bounced up and down as he rammed his dick inside. His hard body was pressed against mine as a pleasuring amount of pain erupted from my body. He leaned down and wrapped his mouth around my breasts, sucking on my dark nipples like they were snacks for him. "Shit!" he yelled out as sweat dripped from his brow. "Fuck!"

Just then, he pulled out and flipped me over onto my stomach. He pressed his hand into the back of my head and buried my face down into the pillow as he stuck his dick back inside of me. With his other hand, he smacked my ass while he mounted me from behind. I yelled as loud as I could into the pillow, my voice muffled by the soft cotton inside.

"Yes!" My voice was muffled. I felt another wave ready to shoot from my vagina as his dick found its way around to every spot that I couldn't reach with my fingers.

It hurt, but the pleasure outweighed the pain. "I'm cuming again," I yelled as I lifted my head from the pillow. My face scrunched up as I bit my lip and grabbed hold of the pillows beside me. Seconds later, I came onto his dick as my heartbeat nearly jumped from my chest. I fixed my mouth to utter ecstasy, but nothing came out. Silent screams of pleasure filled the room as he moaned out loud, and moments later, I felt his warm cum bursting inside of me.

After he finished, he laid down on the couch beside me. There was room enough for the both of us to rest comfortably and as he steadied his breathing with drops of sweat illuminated on his chest in the moonlight, I laid on my back. Just then, my phone rang. It was on the nightstand when I reached over for it. It was a text message from Blake and, just like that, my heart sunk deep into my chest. "What's wrong?" Darryl asked.

I exhaled and put the phone face down on the nightstand. "Nothing. Nothing at all."

"Look, I know you probably already know this, but I love you. Not like, as a sister, either. Like, I love you for real. As in, I can see myself spending the rest of my life with you by my side. That's the truth to why I talk about you so much. You mean a lot to me and I think I was just scared to admit it, but since we just did what we did, I figured I should just keep it a buck with you now."

I hated that he just told me that. I couldn't settle down right now. There was no way that it was possible, especially in my line of work. I cared about Darryl and for that reason alone, I couldn't put him through a relationship with me. Not right now, at least. "Listen, Darryl, I love you too. I really do, but, it's just not the right time to pursue anything like that. I mean, I've got too much going on in D.C. and you wouldn't get the time and attention you need. I don't want to put you through that. You don't deserve it. You deserve someone who can give you the time and attention you need. Not me."

He remained quiet for a few seconds as he laid facing the ceiling. "Darryl?"

"Yeah, I hear you. I wasn't really expecting you to jump into my arms and be with me, you know? I just wanted to put it out there and see what happened after that. I just wanted you to know how I really felt about you, Jae. That's all. No pressure from me though. It's all good. Either way, I'ma still love you."

"And I will still love you, too. But, maybe next lifetime."

He smiled and nodded his head. "Now you quotin' Badu on me, huh?"

"Yeah. It is time for that."

He nodded his head and after that, he wrapped his arms around me and we laid with each other for the rest of the night. I hated that I couldn't stay like this with him. Darryl was special to me in a number of ways and honestly, he would've been the perfect man to compliment me. We complimented each other well and I don't know of any woman that wouldn't want to spend the rest of their lives married to their best friend. That is how it would've been with me and Darryl and I knew it, but it was just bad timing and I had to accept that and just hope that he would be around for me later.

The next day, he took me to the airport. We hugged each other like it was the last time we would see one another. "Until next time," he said, not wanting to let go of my hand.

"Yes. Until next time. I love you, Darryl."

"I love you, too, Jae."

With a smile and a lingering connection, I turned to walk onto the airplane. Away from heaven and back to the hell I was caught in the middle of.

CHAPTER 4

Jae

"**W**here have you been? We have been worried sick about you."

I pushed the door closed as my aunt perked up while she sat on the couch. I rolled my eyes. "Oh, now you want to be concerned about me or anybody outside of you? It is too late for that."

"Damn, Jae. I just wanted to know if you were alright. You weren't answering the calls or anything. Maybe I should just stop caring."

"Even if you did, I wouldn't notice the difference."

I walked past her and into my room. A few minutes later, there was a knock on my door and quickly after that, it swung open. Angie stood on the other side with one eyebrow above the other and her hands propped on her hips. "Um, you didn't have to talk to her like that."

"Like what? She gets on my nerves."

"She was just concerned about you." She pushed the door closed, then sat down on the bed beside me. "But, seriously, where have you been? You were out of pocket for like a day."

"I know. I um, I went to go see Darryl in school."

She pushed her lips to the side of her mouth. "Bull-shitting."

"Nah, I'm serious." I pulled up the itinerary from my email to show the flight to and from his school. "Now what do you have to say?"

"Ok," she said after she saw the email, "so, you did go to visit him. Why did you go though?"

"I just needed to get away. It was too much shit going on here and I needed to step away for a minute. Get a fresh breath of air, you know? And um—" I paused. I didn't know what she was going to say after I told her what me and Darryl did. "We um—we had sex last night."

Her smile slowly shifted into full blown laughter as she

clapped her hands together. "Are you for real? Yall fucked?"

"Yes. Is that such a surprise to you?"

"Nah, it ain't. I mean, honestly, I thought that shit would've happened a long time ago. I know he felt some kind of way about you and I know you feel the same way about him. You've just been to busy to give the nigga a chance."

"Shit, I am still too busy. He tried to get me to get in a relationship with him before I left. I told him I couldn't do it though. I have too much going on."

"Really, Jae? You turned him down? That fine ass nigga?"

"Yeah, I had to. It wouldn't have been right to be with him, knowing the shit I am involved in here. I couldn't hurt him like that. He is too special to me."

She folded both of her legs beneath her. "Maybe you should give it a shot though. You got enough money to step away from this shit for a little while and test the waters with him. Maybe you will like it more than you think. Shit, maybe you can even go back to school and work on getting your degree so you can leave this shit alone for good."

I exhaled and mirrored the way she sat on top of the bed. "Nah, I don't think that is the play right now. There is too much money to be made out here."

"But, how long do you think you can do this shit? You have to have something else planned so you can fall back on it. This won't last forever. Honestly, I think you need to rethink that. Hell, that nigga might even end up in the NBA because from what I hear, he is ballin' in college. Shit, you can get with him and then live the life with all the money and not have to work another day in yo' life."

"It Is all still a gamble. He is not a lock to make it to the league. He ain't fuckin' Kobe Bryant or Lebron or some shit."

"Yeah, but the nigga got G."

"Either way, I don't want to risk that. And besides, I don't want to be dependent on another nigga like that. I want to work for mine and that is what I am doing now." She looked away from me and didn't say a word. Her silence said more than anything she had to say verbally. "Aight. I'll think about it, ok? I'll sleep on it and see if I change my mind."

She stood up from the bed. "Cool. That is all I'm askin'. Just think about it. Don't close that door so fast because I think yall are a perfect fit. For real. You don't find a connection like that too often."

"Yeah. That's what I hear."

The next day, I went to the office to visit Erica. As soon as I got there, I saw Blake in the lobby. I exhaled and froze when I saw him. He stood to his feet and walked over towards me. "Hey. Where have you been?"

"I've um—I've been a little out of pocket. My aunt—she has a drug addiction and she moved back in with me, so I've had my hands full trying to keep her clean, you know? I don't want her to fall back into that lifestyle."

"Oh." His eyebrows wrinkled as he nodded his head.

"What are you here for?"

"I needed to meet with Erica to see if she could smooth things out between us. You weren't talking to me and you've been acting different ever since that thing happened back at my place. You know, with um—" I could tell that he didn't want to revisit the situation. "Anyways, I wanted to see if she could fix it for us, but here you are right now. Maybe I can fix it without talking to her about it."

"Ok."

"So, your aunt has an addiction? I can pay for the rehab if you want me to."

"No, that is not necessary."

"It is. Not only is it something that usually needs intervention, but it is keeping us from talking to each other. Keeping us from seeing each other and that is the very last thing I want to happen. Just let me do this for you. For her. If it can erase the distance between us, I will do it. I will do anything. I insist."

"Blake—"

"You search for a rehab center—no, as a matter of fact, I have a friend of a friend who owns the Second Chance clinic. It is supposed to be the best in D.C. I will set her up there and I won't take no for an answer. I will call you later to get the information I need about her and we will go from there, ok?"

I didn't respond, but he wasn't going to go away unless I agreed with him. I exhaled. "Alright. Thank you, Blake."

"My pleasure. Now, hopefully this opens things up for us again. Are you free tonight? We can talk about the details over dinner."

I reluctantly agreed to meet him for dinner later that

night. Minutes later, he left, and Erica's office door opened. She started to call his name, but she stopped once she didn't see him in the lobby. "He left," I said, walking closer to her.

"I see. Well, I've got an open slot now, so if you are here to see me, you can take his."

I followed her into her office. She switched her hips back and forth until she made it to her side of the desk and sat down. She pushed her glasses onto the bridge of her nose, folded her hands on the table in front of her and looked directly at me. "So, what can I do for you, Jae? What do you need?"

"I want to take on some new clients. I think I need to distance myself from Blake. I feel like I am getting too close to him emotionally."

"Hmm. I see. Yeah, that is definitely going to be a problem for business. Alright. I will see what I can do. In the meantime, just keep him entertained and try to control your emotions. We don't want this to be a smear on what we have going on. All it takes is one disgruntled client for things to start to fall apart."

"Ok. I'm supposed to go out with him tonight. I really don't want to but—"

"You will go. Just stick it out and I'll be working on sending some more clients your way. It won't take long, alright?"

I sighed. I knew this was a part of the business and I had to go along with it. The money was rolling in far too fast for me to just turn away from it. Later that night, I got ready for my date with Blake. He pulled out the red carpet for me. We took the Maybach to a high scale restaurant where nothing on the menu was under $100 dollars.

He sat across from me, fixating on everything I was doing. The candle flickered on the table as soon as he began to speak. "So, I know things are a little awkward between us right now and I get it. I've been trying to do everything I can to make you feel more comfortable with me. Giving you space, trying not to hound you. Just this week, I've given you more money in the last few days than I can recall. But I can't help that I feel like I am losing you."

I took a sip of wine, then gently placed it back down on the table. "I am sorry for being so distant. Like I said, it was more so my aunt than anything else, so I hope that you don't take that the wrong way. But I apologize for my distance. Sometimes I can become reclusive when I get stressed."

He reached over and grabbed my hand on top of the table. "Apology accepted. But can we try not to do that again? I mean, I felt like I was dying when I couldn't talk to you. When I couldn't see you. You are literally giving me air to breathe. I need you."

I forced a facetious smile across my face. "I'll be here for as long as I can."

I couldn't tell him that I was going to start taking other clients. It was the wrong time and he already seemed emotionally vulnerable. I had to keep it quiet for now just to keep the peace.

CHAPTER 5

Blake had been sending me sweet texts all day, telling me how much he missed me and what he wanted to do the next time he saw me. I was more cognizant of having sex with him this time around. I knew where my heart was for him and I didn't want to make things worse. I ignored his texts and looked across the table at my date.

Erica sent me a new client in a matter of days, and this was our first date together. He was a short, handsome, wealthy man in his early thirties. A pleasant smile with deep pockets. I smiled his way as he continued his conversation. "So, I was completely taken back by the fact that I had to donate a few thousand dollars just to make it all go away. But, it was nothing. I did what I had to do and, outside of that, I had money to spare. I'd spent more in a day anyway, so, it was nothing."

I nodded my head and took another sip of my wine. He spoke as if he had to convince me that he had money. He didn't know the game. We only dealt with men who had money. That was a part of the agreement. Just then, I heard a familiar voice. My eyebrows winkled together as I looked to the right. Blake stepped into the restaurant with his wife.

I exhaled and shook my head just as we made eye-contact. He whispered something to his wife, forcing her to turn and walk back through the exit. My heart-beat sped up as he headed in my direction. My date continued bragging on himself without noticing what was coming our way.

"Jae?" Blake said, standing beside our table. He smiled. "What is this about?"

"Hi, Blake. This is Steven. Steven, this is Blake."

Steven extended his hand to Blake, but it was ignored. "Um, can I see you for a second?"

I smiled and removed the napkin off my lap, then placed it to the side of my plate. "Steven, can you excuse me for a moment? I'll be back shortly."

He looked confused by everything, but he didn't fight it. He wiped his mouth. "Ok. But, don't stay gone too long."

I stood up and walked with Blake until we stopped in the hallway near the restrooms. He was visibly bothered, but he did a great job of keeping calm in the middle of it. "What is this about? You are seeing someone else?"

"Yes, I am. Is that a problem? I mean, you have a whole wife at home. She was just here with you before you sent her off somewhere. So, how is it a problem for me but it is alright for you?"

"Because you are not the one who makes the rules here. I have a wife. You knew that from the beginning, but we never spoke about you seeing or dating anyone else. It doesn't work both ways. You are with me. Period."

He reached for my arm, but I quickly snatched it out of his grasp. "Listen, Blake. I don't know what you think this is, but I am on a date with someone else. So, if you don't want me to make a scene and have the police called, I suggest you and your WIFE either find a place to sit in here or go to another restaurant altogether. We are done with this conversation."

I left him standing in the middle of the hallway and made my way back to Steven. "Is everything alright?" he asked as I took my seat.

"Yes. Everything is fine. It was just a misunderstanding. But, what were you saying?"

"Oh, I was just saying that—"

Just then, Blake showed up at the side of our table again. I exhaled and shook my head, then put my hand over my face. I couldn't help but to chuckle a bit at his reaction. It was cute to see someone as jealous of me as he had become. He put his hands on his hips and looked at Steven. "Sir, I don't mean to bother you, but do you know how old she is?"

Steven wrinkled his eyebrows as he looked towards me. "I was under the impression that she was above 18. I mean, I know she looks young but—"

"Fifteen." I stifled my laugh. "She is fifteen. How do I know? She is my niece. Now, I suggest that, if you don't want me to contact my brother, who happens to be a lawyer that lives off putting scumbags like you beneath the prison, then you should probably leave right now."

"Fifteen?" he asked, looking at me. I knew Erica would have a field day with this one. I looked away from him, refusing to respond. I was just about over our date anyway. He had become far too annoying much too fast. Finally, he stood to his feet and wiped his mouth with his napkin. He didn't say a word to me as he tossed it on the table and left the restaurant.

Blake occupied his seat across from me, smiling. "How was that?"

"It was completely uncalled for. You know Erica is going to want to smash your face in."

"There is nothing that a little extra money can't fix. Besides, I can't stomach to see you with another man, so, let this be a lesson to you. Call it providence that I ended up in the same place as you tonight. Some things were just meant to be, and this was definitely one of them, whether you want it to be or not.

I took another sip of my wine and couldn't help but chuckle at everything that had just happened. I quietly appreciated him for saving me from the horrendous date and remained with him for the rest of the evening.

After I got home, I mentioned the rehab to Aunt Jeanie and Angie. They both seemed elated that it had become an option. "Well, who is paying for it?" Angie asked.

"I am. I just feel like it is time to get you some real help, so, that is what I am going to do. I want to see you clean and not have to worry about you going back out into the street to satisfy your addiction. I want you to get the help you need."

She stood up and wrapped her arms around me. I felt tears fall onto my neck as we embraced each other. Angie stood off to the side, smiling. I knew that this would be something that could help strengthen our bond together. I just hated that Blake had to be the one to initiate it all. I guess I just felt that my aunt couldn't be changed for the better, but everyone deserved another chance. Now, it was her time to get that chance.

We released each other. "I'll let you know when every-thing is set up."

"Ok." She wiped tears from her eyes. "thank you so much, Jae. So much."

I smiled at her and Angie, then went to my room and shut the door. I guess breaking away from Blake was going to be harder than I imagined.

Blake

I closed the front door to find my wife seated with her leg folded over her knee and a bottle of wine on the table in front of her. "So, you ditched me for you little girlfriend tonight, huh? You don't need to hide it. The fact that we went out and you literally sent me home after you saw her said enough, and you know what?"

She took a sip of her drink as I stepped into the front room. "Two can play this game. If you are seeing other people so openly, then, I will do the same thing."

She thought that would hurt me, but I had no emotional connection to her anyway. It wasn't like how I felt with Jae. The jealously pumped through my heart red like the blood that was already there. I shrugged my shoulders. "Ok. Do what you need to do. That's your choice."

I walked out of the living room, but she put her glass down and followed me through the house. "It's just like that? You don't care? You send me home because your girlfriend was on a date with another man, but if I go out with someone else, then you don't care?"

"No, I don't. Look, I don't feel the same way for you that I feel about her, ok? Let's just talk facts right now. You can do what you want. You can see who you want. I am not going to fight you over that. We can live our lives together, separately, if that makes sense."

"You know what?! Fuck you!" She shoved me in my back, and I stumbled forward. "Fuck you, Blake! I am sick of you! I am sick of this!" She shoved me again.

I stumbled forward a second time and then turned to face her just as she sent a punch towards my face. I dodged it, then grabbed her hands and pinned her back into the wall. "Have you lost your fucking mind? I let you get away with the shoves, but you have the gall to try to hit me across the face? You need to calm the fuck down before you piss me off and trust me, you don't want to go there with me."

She struggled to get free, but once she realized she was going nowhere, she stopped. "Let me go, Blake."

"Are you done?"

"I said let me go, Blake! You're hurting my wrist!"

"I will when you are calm."

"I am. Fucking. Calm. Now, let me go. Please!" I held her for a moment longer, then stepped away. She fixed her dress back into place, then glared at me. "I am going to get you back for all of this, Blake," she wiped a tear from her eye. "Every time you have cheated in my face with no qualms about the way I feel. You are going to reap each and every last feeling. I promise you that."

"Do you want a divorce? Let's just get a divorce and end this right now because I don't have time for foolishness." She stormed down the hallway, snatched her purse and keys off the counter and left the house. I didn't know what she had up her sleeve, but whatever it was, I didn't have time for it. I needed to get her out of the picture before something else went wrong.

CHAPTER 6

Jae

"Are you ready to go, Aunt Jeanie?"

"Just about, Jae. Just putting the last few things in my bag. I am excited and nervous about this all at the same time."

"You're going to be fine, Aunt Jeanie. This is going to benefit you in the end. But, we will be in the front room. Just let us know when you are ready so we can head out there. We have to be there by 6 pm and it is a 3-hour drive."

"Ok."

I closed the bedroom door and walked to the front room. We decided to send her to a place out of town, far away from the temptation to get lured back into doing drugs. If she stayed in the city, it wouldn't take much for her to find a way out of the building and get to the drugs if she needed a hit. At least, being out of town, we knew she wouldn't have easy access to it.

"You think she is ready for this?" Angie asked as I sat down beside her.

"I guess we will find out one way or the other."

Minutes later, aunt Jeanie stepped out of the room with bags in her hands. "Ok. I am ready to go," she said with a smile.

Moments later, we got up and made our way to the rehab center. It didn't take long for aunt Jeanie to fall asleep in the back seat. Once Angie noticed that she was out, she sparked up a conversation. "So, how are you paying for all of this?"

"With my money, Angie. Why are you even asking me about that?"

"Because. From the looks of the website and everything, this place isn't cheap. I mean, a couple thousand dollars a day? That is not something that most people would fork out just to help someone, let alone Jeanie. You have never been that high on her." She covered her mouth. "Odk, so maybe that was a bad word choice."

I laughed. "You are stupid. But, no. Like I said, sometimes, people deserve a second chance and I realized that I never really gave one to Jeanie. So, I wanted to make sure that her second chance was a good one. Something that could help free her and keep her free for the rest of her life."

"I see. Well, I hope she makes it through this shit. And," she looked at me, "I think I need to switch professions. I mean, this stripping shit pays the bills, but what you are doing? The money you have coming in? That shit will have a bitch set for life. So, what do you do, exactly?"

I didn't want to tell her the specific details. "You just date a few rich men. They give you money for time and attention. That's basically it."

"Bullshit. Men are not cashing hoes out just for 'time and attention.' You gotta' be busin' it wide open for them, or at the minimal, slobbing the shit out of his dick. I refuse to believe that they are just handing you money because you spend time with them on a date or whatever."

"What do you think I am? Some fuckin' hoe or something?" She didn't respond. "Look, I told you what I do. I spend time with lonely, rich men. Men who have fucked over every woman they've ever known to the point that karma has caught up with them and all they can do now is pay money for a woman to spend time with them. That is it. Now, if you have any other assumptions about what the fuck I do, then keep that shit to yourself."

She triggered me. It was one thing to do what I did, but it was another thing when it was thrown in my face for me to see it in my head. On top of that, I knew she would eventually tell Darryl what was going on and I couldn't risk that. In the back of my mind, I felt like we could still be together later in life and I didn't want to say anything to sabotage that. She shrugged her shoulders, then faced the windshield. "Aight, shit, my bad. I see I pressed the wrong button, so, I'ma just leave that shit alone."

We rode in silence for the next few minutes. I hated when I snapped on her like that. I knew she loved me and was just curious about what was going on in my life. I looked at her as she scrolled through her phone. "So, are you talking to anyone? Any boyfriends or anything?"

"Nah, you know most niggas can't handle a stripper

bitch. They can't deal with all the niggas we be around on a daily basis. So, I don't expect to have a nigga right now. I'm just focused on getting this bread, you know? But, what about you and Darryl? Have you talked to him again lately?"

"No, and I haven't made a decision about it yet, either. I've just been thinking. There is a lot to consider. I need to make money right now and I know you know the feeling."

"Yeah, but damn, Jae, how long are we going to do this? How long are you going to do what you are doing? How long am I going to strip? Like, this shit only lasts as long as our bodies are tight, and we look good. I've been thinking about other options. Like, going back to school and shit. Maybe we can both do that."

"Nah, I can't do that. If I go to college, then I have to wait to make money. That is time wasted. I can make money now and skip all the bullshit in between, you know? That is what I want to do. So, at least for right now, that is not an option for me."

She exhaled and faced forward. "Yeah. It is sort of a trap. A punk ass trap."

The ride to the facility was quiet from that point on.

There was so much to say, but neither of us knew how to say it. She was right. We were both in a trap. A fucking trap.

"Alright, aunt Jean, we are here."

She slowly woke up in the back seat as we arrived at the facility. It was the size of a mansion. Four large pillars stretched from the top of the porch to the bottom. The bold green grass blanketed the lawn and people dressed in white clothing stood outside near benches and swings, conversating with each other.

We all got out of the car and looked at what seemed to be a glimpse of heaven. We each grabbed a bag and then walked into the building to check her in. She couldn't stop smiling the whole time. She was directed to her own suite. A room much larger than the one she had at my house, complete with a window view that overlooked the back of the facility. Man-made ponds were sprinkled throughout the yard, as well as gazebos and small bridges to travel over the ponds. "This is beautiful," she said as we looked out the window.

"So, you're going to be alright here, Aunt Jeanie?"

She smiled. "Yes. I will be fine."

"Ok. We promise to visit you at least twice a month on

the weekends. We want you to get better, so, take advantage of everything that they have here, ok?"

"I will." She had tears in her eyes. "Thank you so much, Jae. Thank you so much."

We all embraced each other and after that, me and Angie headed back home. Angie got ready for her shift at the strip club as I laid in my bed, thinking about what I was going to do with my future. Angie really had me thinking about it ever since our conversation in the car. From there, I grabbed my phone to call Blake. I remembered him saying that he would help me sort things out for my future.

"Hello?"

"Blake?"

"Hey, Jae. I was just thinking about you. What's up?"

"I want you to do something for me. I want you to take me places I've never been. I want to see things I've never seen before. I want you to open my eyes so I can see the world in a different way. Maybe—maybe it will help me gain a little more perspective about my life and the way things are going."

"I see." He paused for a moment. "Have you ever been to Paris?"

"No. I've never been."

"Ok. Get ready. I'll have my jet take us over there."

"Now?"

"Yes, now."

CHAPTER 7

We got onto his jet, holding hands as we floated through the sky. Just like that, we were on our way to Paris. I didn't think that he would do something like this for me so fast, but he did, and my heart raced with excitement.

"I think this is a much-needed vacation for the both of us."

"I agree."

"Do you remember the last time we were on a plane with each other?"

He smiled. I knew I triggered the same thoughts as him. He took his hand and slid it onto my thigh. I didn't want to go there with him because I knew that it would deepen my feelings for him even more than what they already were, but I couldn't help it. Moments later, he eased me on top of him as I wrestled his belt buckle loose.

He reclined the seat back as I put my hand into his chest. I wanted to control it. His shorts fell below his waist and hit the ground. I stroked my hand over his dick and bobbed my head up and down on it at the same time. I knew what he liked. I smacked his erected penis on the side of my face a couple of times, then slid it back into my mouth, wrapping my lips around it tightly on its way in and out. He reached forward and pulled my shirt over my head, exposing my bra. I slid one hand back and unstrapped it as my titties fell free from their traps. I licked his shaft and slobbed on it, then jacked him off as I watched his eyes roll to the back of his head.

Without warning, I took his penis and slid it in the middle of my breasts. I squeezed them together as I moved my chest up and down. The top of his dick jabbed me in the bottom of my throat as he titty-fucked me.

He grabbed my breasts and thrusted his pelvis up and down. He picked up his speed, but I quickly removed my titties from his dick and slid my mouth back onto it. I could feel his pre-cum squeezing out of him as he yelled out in ecstasy.

He reached forward and pushed my head back down onto his dick. It reached the back of my throat and forced me to gag as I removed it from my mouth. Long streams of pre-cum stretched from the tip of his penis to my lips as I moved it away. I stroked his dick with both hands as he pounded the cushions on the couch. As soon as I felt his dick jump, I quickly put my mouth back on him. He shot his cum inside of my mouth as I moaned. It dripped down the side of my face and onto to my breasts as my mouth filled up with it. When he was done, I stood up in front of him and dropped my pants to the ground.

His dick was still hard as I slid on top of him; my pussy was already soaked, so he slid right in. I quickly hopped off of him. "Oh my God," I said as I felt the pleasuring pain from his length. I grinded on top of him while his dick brushed against my clit, sending a rush of moisture from the inside of me. I ran my hands over the ripples on his chest as I looked down at his waist. His dick was just beyond my belly, stretching upwards towards my breasts.

I wanted it back inside of me, and as I grinded on top of

him, he eased it back in. He lifted me off the mattress and laid me on my back and from there, he moved inside of me slowly. His waist moved back and forth like he was in rhythm to a beat inside of his head. His abs flexed right in front of me as he used his stomach muscles like he was slow dancing.

He sent his tongue onto the edge of my ear and licked it softly, making a trail from there to my collarbone as my legs tightened around him. He slid his hand onto my ass, gripping a handful of it while he moved on top of me. With his other hand, he stroked my hair and kissed me softly on the lips as if it was the last time he was going to see me. The last time he was going to hold me. As he pumped, I dug my nails into his back.

He placed his hands on the mattress and pushed himself up while I locked my legs around him. His mouth slid onto my nipples, caressing them with his tongue. He bit his lip and sped up. My titties bounced up and down on my chest as I closed my eyes and reached for pillows to cover my face.

He lifted my up and laid me on the floor of his jet. I could feel the propellers vibrate the cabin floor beneath me, adding to the pleasure that rumbled through my body. I pulled him on top of me. He grabbed my legs and pinned them behind my head. His dick pierced my stomach as vibrations sent waves through my body. I bit my lip, trying to muffle my screams as I yelled out in a pain and pleasure cocktail as I reached down and stroked my clit when I was on the verge of coming. "Aaaaaaah! Yes!"

He flipped me over and before I could prepare myself, he shoved his long dick inside of me and smacked my ass. I gripped the edge of the bed. "Shit!" I yelled out as he grabbed a handful of my hair. He had me pinned against the floor, and seconds later, I came. We laid, life-less, on top cabin floor as I faced the ceiling. Just when I vowed not to go that route with him again, it happened. He had me and I wasn't sure if I was going to ever be able to let go.

As soon as we landed, his servants removed our luggage from the jet and placed them into the vehicle that was waiting for us near the runway. The air was different across seas. I could tell that I was no longer at home just by the scent of everything. "It is beautiful here, Jae. But, you haven't even touched the tip of the iceberg yet." He extended his hand for me. "Come on. Let's go. The city is awaiting."

We climbed in to his vehicle and with that, we were out

of the airport. I took snapshots of the statues and land-marks as we drove through the city. We just landed, but I was already amazed at everything I saw. I snapped pictures and sent them back home to Shayla and Angie. "I see you are living the life, bitch," Shayla responded. "Shit. I need to find me a nigga that will fly me across the fucking world, too. Shit."

I closed my phone as he slid his arm around me. "I can't wait for you to see the city. I guarantee that you will not want to leave. I was the same way when I came here the very first time."

We arrived at the five-star hotel. The bellhop immedi-ately removed our bags from the car and placed them on a small gurney, then wheeled them to the elevator in front of us. The elevator stopped on the twenty-ninth floor of the building; a penthouse suite. The doors opened and revealed a canopy bed in the middle of the room.

Champagne bathed in buckets of ice on top of the dresser. The white linen made it seem as if we were in heaven. The floors sparkled and the marble countertops in the bathroom reminded me of Blake's place back home. They had similar décor. "You're right. I think I am going to love it."

I stepped out onto the balcony. The evening lights had just set in. The downtown skyline looked picture perfect as he came outside and stood behind me on the balcony. "We will have to make this a normal occasion. It is time that we went places outside of the U.S. Maybe we will try Bora-Bora next. I know you will love it there even more, but for now, we should hurry. I have dinner reservations for us in the city."

I smiled and gladly too his hand as we walked out of the hotel room and back down to the car. We arrived at a restaurant about fifteen minutes away from our hotel. After dinner, we strolled through the city. Soft music played through the speakers outside of the Eiffel tower. We stopped right in front of it and he held me in his arms. "You know, I can really see myself with you down the line," he said as he beheld me. "I want us. I want this, whatever we have, to go as far as it possibly can. You are everything to me."

"Really? Well, do you plan on leaving your wife to make that happen?"

"I'm sorry?"

"You know you can't have us both, Blake. And, if you see yourself with me down the line, then of course she cannot be in the picture."

He smiled, then pulled me in for a kiss. I could tell that he didn't want to answer the question or even discuss the topic. That alone made me feel as if what I was doing was a lost cause. There was no point of me allowing my feelings to continue to grow with him, knowing that he quite possibly never planned on leaving his wife for me. It was all talk. Pipe dreams.

After our lips released, I wanted to know more. I had to ask him more. "So, when was the last time you were here?"

"I came here with my wife a few years ago."

My eyebrows wrinkled together. "Your wife?"

"Yes. Clarissa. I—" He paused, knowing that he had just said too much. With his response, the air had been sucked out of the room. "That doesn't bother you, does it?"

I stepped away from him. "Can we go back to the room now?"

"Jae? Come on. You asked me when was the last time I came and I simply—"

"The hotel, Blake. Please."

He exhaled, and with that, we made our way back to the

room. I didn't say a word to him as I went to the guest room in the penthouse. He knocked on the door minutes later. "Are you going to stay in here?"

I shrugged my shoulders as I kept my eyes glued to the phone. After he left, I scrolled through my text messages until I landed on Darryl's name. He was the only person that could get my mind off the mess I was going through with Blake. My feelings for him were strong enough to overcome anything I had built for Blake.

"Hello?"

I smiled. "Hey, Darryl. Are you busy?"

"No. I just got up and I'm getting ready to go to class. What's up?"

"Class? You mean star athletes like you still have to go to class?"

"Nah, we don't, but I'm going. I need my degree just in case shit falls apart for me with the whole basketball thing. That is not a lock, so I'm taking advantage of shit while I am in school. I have to. I've been given too much to just let shit fall apart."

"Yeah, I hear you. But, I was just calling to say hey, I guess. You can call me later."

"Nah, nah, it's cool. We can talk. Shit, if I end up missing a class, it ain't a big deal. I've only missed it a few times this semester anyway. But, what's good? You know I can't resist talking to you."

We sat on the phone for the next hour, talking about what happened between us when I came to visit him a few days ago. It only took a phone call to make my feelings for Darryl come back to the forefront. I couldn't deny how I felt about him and how he made me feel. The more I spoke to him, the more I felt like I should've been with him from the beginning.

Suddenly, there was a quick knock on the door before Blake came in. I quickly ended the call but kept it near my ear to give the appearance that I was still on the phone. "Um, yes?"

"Who were you talking to? I stood outside the door, so I know it is someone special to you."

"Darryl? He is just a friend."

"Just a friend? Reminiscing the way you two were just reminiscing? Laughing? Saying how much you missed being around him? I call bullshit on that. I told you that seeing anyone else is not an option for you. Didn't I?"

"Are you serious right now? You have a wife back in the

U.S. and you have the nerve to try to dictate who I can and cannot talk to? This has to be a joke. Somebody please tell me where the candid cameras are at. This is seriously a joke, right, Blake? Right? A joke?"

"I will tell you what the joke is. If you don't take heed to what I am saying, I will cut you off. You know what that means? No more money. And, on top of that, I will snatch your aunt out of that rehabilitation center. You can test me if you want to, but all it takes is a phone call. You cut that shit out right now or I will make good on my word. That is not a threat; that is a promise."

He slammed the door closed on his way out. I couldn't believe that Blake had just chosen to flex like this. I never thought he would say or do anything like that to me. "He is just a friend, Blake!" I yelled through the door. He didn't come back. I sunk into my bed and exhaled, feeling more trapped now than I had at any point before.

~

Blake

I CLIMBED into bed upset and full of jealousy. There was no way that I would be able to take Jae seriously in a relationship because of her past, but at the same time, I didn't want her connecting with anyone else in that way. I knew it was hypocritical and wrong of me to be so possessive over Jae, but something had to change.

I thought about Carissa and how maybe the best thing to do was just to divorce her and let her live her life so I could live mine. I knew she wouldn't sign the papers though. She had a reason for putting up with my issues and still sticking around. It would be too hard to get her to see things my way. I turned over on the other side and put my head on the pillow, doing everything in my power to keep from getting up to go back in the room with Jae. I had to figure out how to fix this before I ended up losing her. I just had no idea how to do it.

CHAPTER 8

Jae

The next day, Blake apologized for how he acted the night before. I knew I had to accept his apology if I didn't want this trip to go sour. He had all the power and he could very well leave me out in Paris and return home. After last night, I didn't trust him to treat me the way he had been.

He took me shopping. I went from rack to rack, searching for things to string together from a fashion standpoint. It seemed like that was the only thing that gave me life. Blake stood beside me and leaned against one of the racks. "So, I see how you are cheesing while you put together outfits. I know that you enjoy shopping, but it seems like you are having more fun putting things together."

I held up a shirt. "Yes, I do. I think it is just a pastime of mine, you know? I enjoy fashion."

"A pastime? You know that people can make good money off that. Buyers. Have you heard of it?"

I put the shirt back on to the rack. "Yes, I have. But, I know I have to go to college for something like that. I just don't have the time for it."

"Oh, yes you do. You are young. You have all the time in the world right now. How about this? I'll send you to school. I'll send you to the best fashion school out here and then you can get your degree and pursue your dreams. How does that sound?"

The last thing I wanted was to make another attachment to Blake. He already had too much of me and if I allowed him to pay for my school and I did something he didn't like, there was nothing that would stop him from taking me out the same way he threatened to take my aunt out of rehab. "Yeah, maybe I will look into that, but I don't need you to pay for it. I can handle it myself."

"What? I can send you to the best school that money can buy. Now, I know you are a probably a little apprehensive because of how things went last night, but I promise you that there will be no strings attached. I want you to succeed in life. You asked me to show you different things and now that you have seen them, I want you to have them. I want you to go as far as you can go in life and if I can help you do that, then I will. Just let me. Let me do this for you. Please."

"I'll think about it, Blake. I'll think about it."

He smiled. "That is better than nothing. I'll take it."

We stayed in Paris for another week before we decided to go back to the states. He opened my eyes to a possible career in fashion, but I was just unsure as to whether I wanted to take him up on his offer. We went back to his place. When we got there, the door was unlocked. I looked at Blake as he wrinkled his eyebrows together, but that was it. We walked inside and after he closed the door behind us, he scooped me off the floor and carried me up to his room.

I pressed my body against him until he backed into the wall. I smiled, then wrestled with his shorts until they plopped onto the floor. I stroked his dick until it hardened up and as I glanced at them, a smirk danced across his face. I softly moved my hand back and forth over it until it hardened stiff like a board. I lifted myself on my tiptoes and kissed him on the lips. His tongue found its way inside my mouth, tasting like the expensive champagne that we both had been drinking for the past hour. I felt his hand cup my ass before he smacked it and gripped it again.

I moved my lips off his and reached to untie the top of my bathing suit. The straps fell off my shoulders, exposing my breasts. My nipples poked out like tiny rockets. My vagina pulsated, waiting for the second that he would slide his long dick into to me. I replayed this scene in my mind from the day we met, and now, it was going to happen. I'd waited long enough. He leaned down and pressed his lips against my neck, slithering his tongue on my flesh like a snake. His hand slid into my bikini, and I felt his finger move in and out of my vagina. I was already soaked, and it wasn't from the water we had just gotten out of.

Suddenly, he grabbed my thighs and lifted me up, pinning my back against the wall until he slid his dick inside of me. My eyes rolled to the back of my head. My walls were tight because I hadn't had sex in so long. "Fuck," he said as he slowly slid into me with my back pinned against the wall. My mouth hung open, but no words escaped. He pulled out of me and went back in. I could feel his dick in my stomach as I wrapped my arms around his neck and kissed him deeply. Soon after that, he picked up his pace. My moans turned into screams of ecstasy as he picked up his speed. My nails dug into his flesh, creating hieroglyphic marks all over his back.

He bit his lip and lifted my legs higher into the air as he kept me pinned against the walls with ease. Suddenly, he removed me from that position and threw me onto the bed. My body bounced on the soft mattress. He grabbed my legs and flipped me over onto my stomach, then grabbed my waist and pulled me back onto his dick. He smacked my ass and pushed my head down into the mattress. That's when it started to hurt more, but the pain was pleasure. I yelled into the mattress as the covers muffled my screams. I tried to steady my breathing as his dick pierced me. He grabbed my arms and pulled them backwards as he fucked me from behind.

My titties flopped around in front of me with all the sudden movements. A hurricane of cum flowed from between my legs as he stuck his deep further inside of me. "Yes! Yes!" I yelled for him to keep going as I repeatedly came on his dick. He grunted and smacked my ass again as he climbed on top of me and pounded me into the mattress. He fucked the shit out of me, and it was exactly what I needed.

After I left his place, I headed home. Angie arrived at the same time from her night working at the club. I twisted the key in the lock as she had a smile on her face. "Why are you so happy? You must've got some dick."

"Girl, please, ain't nobody smiling just for some dick. I can get that any time I want. I am smiling because as of today, I am no longer showing my ass and titties for money. I quit!"

My eyes popped open as we walked into the house. "For real? You quit?"

"Hell yeah. I told them muhfuckas to kiss my ass on the way out, too. Fuck that shit. I am going back to school to enroll in a nursing program. I think that is what I want to do with my life."

"For real? Damn. Maybe it is a sign?"

We sat down on the couch as she continued. "A sign for what?"

"That I need to take my ass back to school for fashion merchandising so I can be a buyer. When I was gone, I realized that fashion is something that drives me. It is a passion of mine."

"Shit, I could've told you that myself. So, are you going back? Is it official?"

"Pretty much. I just have to choose the school and after that, I'm off."

"Heeeeeey, now! Look at us! We decided to make a change at the same time. This shit is meant to be!"

"Yeah, it has to be meant. It has to."

We gave each other a hug as we sat in the front room, then decided to go to breakfast with mimosas to celebrate. For the first time in my life, it seemed as if things were finally going down the right path not just for me, but for the both of us.

CHAPTER 9

"So, I've decided to go to school. I decided to do it last night."

"Word? For real?"

"Yes! I am so excited and nervous at the same time. I figured I would call you to see if you could help me with the process, you know? Help me maneuver through it all."

"Oh, yeah, no doubt. You know I got you!" Darryl seemed just as excited as me when I told him my plans. I could hear the smile in his voice as he continued the conversation. "You know what? You should just come to my school. Yeah, that would be dope. I saw you looking at all the sororities and shit when we were walking through campus. You can get with one of them and just enjoy the college life, you feel me? I know you would love it. I can get you hooked up with one of the counselors and they will get you right."

"Nah, Blake said I should go to a school that specializes in fashion since that is what—" I froze. I couldn't believe that I allowed his name to slip out of my mouth. Up until this point, I had been painstakingly careful about what I said around Darryl, but I guess my excitement got the best of me this time around.

"Who? Blake? Who is that?"

"Um—he is nobody, Darryl."

"Obviously he is somebody if you are taking that kind of advice from him. Who is he? Is he the reason you don't want to settle down into a relationship with me?"

"Stop it, Darryl. Because, if you want to be real, you didn't even like me until I started changing my look. The way you held me when I came to visit you at your school? You never did that before until you saw how I—"

"Nah, nah, Jae, you can stop that shit right now because I've always loved you. I was just too shy to say something it about it before. But, if I didn't love you, why do all my brothers know who you are? How did they know exactly who you were before you even said a word to them? I've loved you since we were kids and that shit is real, so don't try to act like my feelings for you didn't come until I saw how you looked recently because that is bullshit. My love for you is genuine."

He was right. Maybe he did love me well before he saw me at his school. I just thought he was talking shit before, but I was wrong. After a long pause, he spoke again. "Are you fucking him?"

"What?"

"Are you fucking him?"

"Darryl, seriously? Because that is none of your fucking business."

He exhaled. I could feel him slipping away from me. "You know what? You're right. It ain't none of my business. None of this shit is, so, you keep getting your advice from that nigga and leave me out of it. I wish you the best with all that college shit, oh, and whatever the fuck you got goin' on with that nigga. Leave me the fuck out of it."

"Darry—"

He hung up the phone before I could say anything to him. I shook my head and put the phone on the bed. I wanted to call him back, but I knew he wouldn't answer. When he was mad, I just had to let him be mad until he got over it.

It wasn't until he came home two weeks later for spring break that I was able to talk to him again. He surprised me when I came home and he was already in the living room with Angie. Angie stood up. "Hey sis," she said, smiling, "surprise!"

I looked at Darryl. He stood to his feet with a slight smile on his lips and his arms open for a hug. I smiled and fought tears as I walked into his arms and embraced him. "Damn it feels good to hold you again," he said as he pulled me closer to him. We released each other. "Shit, this is a nice spot though, for real. But, how can you afford this? I mean, I know you don't—"

All of a sudden, he paused. He looked at Angie, but she looked in another direction before he fixed his attention back on me. "Wait a minute—how are you affording this?"

"My money."

"Doing what?"

"Working."

"You don't have a job to afford a spot like this. This is fucking luxury, Jae. Look at this shit. This is fucking penthouse style living. Loft and shit. How—" He smiled and shook his head. "You know what? I'ma just leave. I ain't about to be here for you like this. Fuck that."

He walked out the front door as I glared at Angie. "Why the fuck did you bring him here, Angie!"

I darted out of the room in the middle of her sentence and rushed down to catch up with Darryl before he could get to his car. "Tell me that some nigga is not payin' for you to live here. Tell me that you are not fuckin' a nigga just to pay your fuckin' bills, Jae. Please tell me that shit! Please!"

"Darryl, is not what you think."

"So, the woman I am in love with is not trickin' off a nigga just so he can—"

I reached my hand up as far as it could go and slapped him across the face. "I will not just stand here and let you disrespect me, Darryl! I will not!"

"Then tell me the truth! Tell me what the fuck is goin' on so we can set this shit straight. What is more important? Doin' whatever the fuck you are doing to get money, or keepin' it a buck with me? Huh?"

I couldn't respond. I wasn't ready to give it up and I wasn't ready to be honest with him. Blake had too much control over me. I hung my head. "I'm sorry, Darryl. I'm sorry."

He shook his head. "Yeah. Just what I fuckin' thought."

I watched him get into his car and sped out of the parking lot as I watched a blurry version of his car drive away until he was out of sight.

CHAPTER 10

The next morning, I woke up to the smell of breakfast. In the kitchen, Angie started cooking breakfast. Eggs, bacon and pancakes sat on top of the table as soon as I walked in. "Hey, boo. Look, I know you had a rough day last night and I'm blaming myself for bringing Darryl over here. I didn't know he knew anything about Blake or whatever. He called me last night after he left and told me about the name you mentioned to him a little while ago."

I exhaled and sat down in the chair. "Don't worry about that, Angie. I can't keep shit hidden for long. I love Darryl, I really do, but I can't keep him around, especially knowing what I am involved in. That is the reason why I couldn't get involved with him to begin with. I've just got too much shit goin' on."

She grabbed a plate and put eggs, bacon and pancakes on it for me, then slid it on top of my placemat. The food looked delicious, but I was sick to my stomach because lost Darryl the night before. I couldn't even touch it.

She exhaled and sat down beside me at the table. "Listen, I know that you love Darryl. I can look at you and tell that you have been crying all night because of what happened. So, and I know you don't want to talk about it, but, do you think the money is worth the risk of losing someone like Darryl? I mean, like I been sayin', a love like that doesn't come around often. Hell, it doesn't come around at all for most of us, so, when you find it, you gotta' hold onto it. At least, that is what I think."

I shrugged my shoulders. She made sense, but I really didn't feel like thinking about the two right now. I was still in pain from losing my best friend. I didn't want to think about anything else. My heart couldn't take it. "Listen, what if you come with me today an enroll in an LPN program? We can stop by a college admissions office and see what you will need to get in. That way, you won't have to depend on Blake and you can slowly start breaking your ties to him. What do you think?"

"I don't know, Angie. I just don't know. I am thinking about way too much to let that weigh me down, too. I just need a moment. Please, just give me a minute to myself. Thank you for breakfast though."

She nodded her head. "Ok. I will leave you to yourself."

She got up, put some food on her plate and then went in the front room to watch television. I looked at my phone, hoping that Darryl's name would pop up from a text message, but I knew that was no use. The only person to hit me up over the last few hours had been Blake and right now, he was the last person I wanted to see.

I heard Shayla's voice in the back of my head, warning me not to fall in love with any of the clients. I had to find that out the hard way because of what I had been going through with Blake, but she never told me that love, in general, would be hard to have as well. I wanted Darryl, but I couldn't just let go of what I had with Blake.

I looked at the plate of food in front of me and grabbed a fork, but my appetite escaped me. I pushed the plate back and stood to my feet just as I heard Angie's voice call me from the living room. "Um, Jae? You might want to come in here and check this out. Like, right now!"

I walked into the living room as she held her plate in her hand with her mouth gaped open as she watched the television. "Look," she said, nodding her head towards the screen.

"What is it?" I asked as I looked in that direction.

I squinted my eyes and moved closer to the television as one of the entertainment news stations aired what was going on. "Here, we have an unknown woman with who seems to be billionaire playboy Blake Austin. Now, the picture is blurry, so we can't distinguish if it is him exactly, but it surely seems like it is."

"What the fuck is this?" I said as I sat down beside her on the couch.

"It looks like you were fuckin' Blake at his crib and now, everybody in the fuckin' city knows. That is what it looks like."

"Shit! Fuckin' shit! That is us! That is when we came back from Paris a couple weeks ago! What the fuck?! How did this shit get out?!"

"I don't know, but um, this is about to cause a whole fuckin' mess and you know it. Damn, Jae. Got damnit."

I sat in horror as the news continued replaying the still picture on the screen. I thought about Darryl. I thought about what this would mean for me, Blake and the agency. I thought it about it all and there nothing that I could've done to prepare me for something like this. At a time when I was moments away from having it all, I could literally be stripped of everything that mattered to me.

FIND out what happens next in Secrets Of A Sugar Baby Book 3! Available Now!

FOLLOW Mia Black on Instagram for more updates: @authormiablack

SECRETS OF A SUGAR BABY 3

Jae's life is turned upside down when her secret relationship with Blake is exposed in the most devastating way.

Jae doesn't know if she will ever be able to make up for what happened, but the one thing she can do is find out who revealed her shocking secret.

Find out what happens in part three of Secrets Of A Sugar Baby!

To find out when Mia Black has new books available, **follow Mia Black on Instagram: @authormiablack**